NICK JR.
DORA the EXPLORER

Just Like Dora!

by Alison Inches
illustrated by Dave Aikins

Ready-to-Read

Simon Spotlight/Nick Jr.

New York   London   Toronto   Sydney

Based on the TV series *Dora the Explorer*® as seen on Nick Jr.®

SIMON SPOTLIGHT
An imprint of Simon & Schuster Children's Publishing Division
1230 Avenue of the Americas,
New York, New York 10020
Copyright © 2005 Viacom International Inc.

6 8 10 9 7
Library of Congress Cataloging-in-Publication Data
Inches, Alison.
Just Like Dora! / by Alison Inches.—1st ed.
p. cm. — (Ready-to-read. Pre-level 1 ; #8)
"Based on the TV series Dora the Explorer as seen on Nick Jr."
Summary: Dora leads her friends on an expedition that ends at an ice cream party.
ISBN 0-689-87675-0
[1. Explorers—Fiction.] I. Dora the explorer (Television program) II. Title. III. Series.
PZ7.I355Fo 2004
[E]—dc22
2004010742

Hi! I am Dora.

Do you like surprises?

Then follow me!

Hop across the rocks!

Hop! Hop! Hop!

Splash in the water!

Just like me!

Row across the lake!

Row! Row! Row!

Slide down the hill!

Just like me!

Are we there yet?

Not yet!

Swing on the vines!

Swing! Swing! Swing!

Jump over the logs!

Just like me!

Here we are!

Guess what we see!

An ice-cream party!

Yummy!

We did it!